ADVENTURES OF ROOP

THE GHOST OF AUNT MATRIX

BY

DR HARMEET KAUR BHALLA

Published in 2022
Becomeshakspeare.com

One Point Six Technologies Pvt Ltd
119-123, 1st floor, Building No. J2, Wadala East,
Wadala Truck Terminal,
Mumbai, Maharashtra- 400037, India
T: +91 8080226699

Wordit Art Fund helps deserving authors publish their work by providing monetary support. To apply for funding, please visit us at www. BecomeShakespeare.com

ISBN - 978-93-5667-166-9

CONTENTS

1. CHAPTER ONE..5

2. CHAPTER TWO..10

3. CHAPTER THREE...15

4. CHAPTER FOUR..18

5. CHAPTER FIVE..22

6. CHAPTER SIX...27

7. CHAPTER SEVEN..31

8. CHAPTER EIGHT...37

9. CHAPTER NINE..40

10. CHAPTER TEN..45

SCHOO
SCHOOL BUS

CHAPTER ONE

It was a thunderous night with the waves splashing against the rocks when the bus reached the small city of Travancore. The children had travelled a distance of three hundred kilometres from Madurai to Travancore. They quickly wore their jackets and anxiously jumped from the small bus as their Maths teacher Mr Single called out their names.

Two tall guards with thick moustaches opened the gate. They counted them, got their signatures done in a register and finally allowed them to enter.

The four girls, Roop, Ruhi, Juhi, and Vanya, and four boys, Harsh, Aram, Asin and Daksh, of class six, were selected to live with the country's greatest Mathematician Pompey Plus. They would learn mathematical tricks and puzzles while staying in his Cubic bungalow for five days.

They were accompanied by a driver, conductor, two teachers, Mrs Housy, Mr Single and a peon Smarty.

Roop was the first to run, and she almost dashed into her teacher.

"Sorry, Ma'am."

A curly-haired young boy in a long black coat and pyjamas came up to the gate, "The school children of THE WORDSWORTH SCHOOL…come…. come…. I am 'Metre' son of 'Centimetre'. Sir is waiting for you."

All the children started laughing at hearing his name.

Mr Housy gave Roop an angry stare as she stood near the enormous green iron gate and shouted, "Come inside, all of you and Roop, don't try to create any mischief." Her voice echoed in the hills.

Mrs Housy gave a stern look to the children when they started giggling.

All the boys and girls gathered to look at the mysterious mathematical house. It had walls touching the sky. The colourful house had signs of plus, minus, square and cubes.

All the children were amazed, and they exclaimed, "Wow! just Wow!"

They stood holding each other's hands while

Roop rubbed her eyes, "Mam, this looks like a perfect mathematical haunted house, and it seems as if nobody lives here."

Smarty, their thirty-year-old peon dark complexioned with blonde hair, came walking like a duck and stood in front of all.

"Hmm…hmm…What is all this? You study maths…. plus……. multiply…. I have never seen such a house."

After crossing the narrow path in the garden, they reached the main door, which too was tricky. Meter opened the door, and the house had everything in the shape of triangles, squares, and circles.

"Please be seated, all of you…. meet my uncle, and then we shall have dinner." They sat on the chairs and waited for Pompey.

After a few minutes, a tall man with long hair, thick spectacles and loose clothes entered.

"Hello, children!" he waved both his hands.

The children stood up and wished him, "Good Evening, Sir." He sat down with them, and they introduced themselves one by one.

"I hope you love the subject Maths. Do you know we can play with numbers? You will learn secrets which no one has come across. I will start the classes tomorrow early morning at five o'clock. Be ready, all of you."

The school staff and children were taken to their respective rooms, and within half an hour, they returned for dinner.

The two cooks served unique dishes at the buffet.

The names of dishes were written on small cards, and it all seemed so comical. Ruhi held Juhi's hand and said, "Oh my God, just see the names…. Circled Potato Curry, Square Vegetable special, Baked Oval Aubergines, Triangle Chapati and Chocolate Ice cream cubes."

"Awesome, names," said Asin holding the triangle chapati.

They enjoyed the sumptuous dinner, and Pompey plus proved to be a good host.

"Ma'am, please take us for a walk as we want to see the sea in moonlight," said Roop excitedly after dinner.

Metre interfered, "You can go in the morning as there are high tides at night in the sea. You can play in the front area of the garden. Don't go in the backyard as there are no proper lights."

It was almost midnight till the children played hide and seek in the vast area. The garden had neat hedges and giant trees.

Roop searched for a place to hide when she heard strange sounds from a small dark cottage in the backyard. She remembered that Meter had warned them not to go there. Someone was calling her with a heavy voice, "Come…come….my child. I was waiting for you all. You will not go back now. You are trapped."

CHAPTER TWO

A woman with loose grey hair, an extra-long nose, long hands, and a dirty white gown called her from an open glass window in the small backyard house. It was probably a one-roomed house with stained walls and surrounded by dried leaves on all sides.

She stammered while speaking, "Children…. you…..mathematicians…I will kill you….come…so many have come again….I will eat all of you."

Her voice was not clear. Roop didn't look back but rather ran as fast as she could as she was alone. She had heard stories of ghosts but was not afraid. She wanted to tell her friends, but she thought it was better to ask Meter.

She returned with a blank white face and caught hold of Ruhi's hands. Her friends wanted to ask her something but she kept a finger on her lips.

They all played for a while and then retired to their rooms. The four girls and their teacher were in a single room. Roop's room had a huge glass window. All of them said their prayers on the bed before going to sleep.

When the two girls awoke to someone knocking at the glass window, it was midnight. In the ghostly silence, only the tick-tock of the clock could be heard. Ruhi, Juhi and Mrs Housy were fast asleep.

Roop whispered in Vanya's ear, "Can you hear the strange sound?"

They didn't want to wake up Mrs Housy as she was having a peaceful sleep and snoring with her nose going right and then left. They smiled on seeing her.

Roop and Vanya got down from the bed and walked up to the window. A heavy black curtain covered the window. As the knocking continued and the girls drew the curtains slowly.

A lady in a white gown with a white face pointed her sharp long nails at them. She turned back after seeing them and left waving her long hands in the air.

Roop shouted, "Look, she is the same lady!"

"Who is she?" asked Vanya, almost fainting on the sofa.

Roop brought a glass of water for Vanya and pulled

back the curtain.

"I saw the same lady when we were playing in the garden. She was calling me. She wanted to kill all of us."

Vanya started sobbing and said, "I think there is a ghost in this house. It would be of great help if you told Mrs Housy…..Oh! I am afraid of ghosts. We should go back."

Roop peeped from the space between the curtains, but no one was there. The same house was visible from the window, but the door was shut.

"My God! She has vanished."

Vanya started sweating and said in a low voice, "She was running. I saw her…..in the white gown…. long hands."

In the meantime, Ruhi and Juhi came yawning and asked, "What happened? Why are you crying, Vanya?"

Vanya held their hands and said, "Ghost…. white ghost…. Pompey plus lives in a haunted house."

"Let us tell Mrs Housy."

Roop interfered, "No…. let her sleep…. we will tell her in the morning."

CHAPTER THREE

The girls couldn't sleep, and they woke up at 4 a.m. as they had to be ready for their first mathematics class. Their teacher accompanied them to the dining room. Mr Single entered with the boys holding their notebooks and pencil boxes.

The students started whispering and giving strange looks to each other. Harsh and Asin were the bold ones, and they moved with Roop and Juhi towards the huge window.

Vanya pointed her index finger with her fingers trembling, "See, that is the cottage. She lives there."

All the boys moved towards the window and pushed each other so that they could have a clear look. They started whispering "Ghost.....Ghost," when Mr Single came and instructed, " What rubbish are you speaking? Get back to your places. The class is about to begin."

Roop and Vanya had already told Ruhi and Juhi about the strange happenings of the previous night. They smiled on seeing Meter.

Mrs Housy poured tea, and the students were served chocolate shakes with doughnuts. Mr Pompey plus entered and ordered them to follow him.

All of them got up from their seats and followed him. They crossed a dark room to reach the basement. Mr Pompey ordered them to wait. He pushed the huge heavy iron door and entered first.

It was a huge old-fashioned classroom with benches, chairs and blackboards. On the walls were huge portraits of Mathematicians.

"Students you should have a look at these great mathematicians. They are our heroes and have laid the foundations," instructed Pompey and all of them started reading their life story which too was written in the right-hand corner.

Roop suddenly stopped in front of a portrait of a young lady. On, a closer look, she found her nose quite long. The name and details were written in one corner.

She started reading "Mrs Sylvia Matrix was born in 1955 in Pune. Her English mother and South Indian father took great care of her education. She was a brilliant child with a special love for mathematics. After studying in the college, she got a special post at The Mathematical Institute of Delhi. She holds a special place in the field of Algebra today….."

She tried to read further but it was scribbled with a sketch pen. She called Vanya and made her look at the portrait, "Come here…..look at her….she resembles the ghost…but I am not sure."

Mr Pompey interfered, "Well my children…..don't stick to one photo….gather knowledge about all."

Both the girls said together, "Yes Sir," and moved forward.

They looked back again with a suspicious look. She started thinking that if she placed white hair instead of black Mrs Matrix would look quite similar to the ghost.

After ten minutes all the students took their seats and the class began.

CHAPTER FOUR

The lecture was quite exhausting as Mr Pompey did not give a break. It went on for four hours. The students sighed relief the moment Mr Pompey finally put down his chalk and duster.

Mr Pompey Plus was the first to leave and Roop was the first one to stand up. She indicated the rest to pay attention to the portrait.

All the students gathered near Roop as she had some important information for them.

"Who is she? asked Daksh and Harsh pointing towards the picture of the lady mathematician.

Ruhi started reading, "Mrs Sylvia Matrix." She said blinking her eyes, "I have never heard her name."

Roop almost whispered, "She has a nose similar to that of the ghost."

Ruhi spoke with eyes wide open, "My….my….she is known to Sir. Is she dead? Is her ghost living in this house?"

"I think Mr Pompey practices witchcraft also," said Vanya looking meticulously at the photograph.

In the meantime, Mr Pompey returned, "Children are not obeying my orders….come on….it's lunchtime."

All of them stood straight as if nothing had happened and followed him.

The children were famished and rushed to have their lunch.

After lunch Mr Single told the students, "Children we are now going to the sea beach……be ready."

The children screamed, "Ye….ye…. the famous Dolphin beach."

"Yes, it is just behind Mr Pompey's house," said Smarty.

The students gathered near the main gate when Meter came running, "Mr Plus has ordered that I should accompany you as there are several lanes which you have to cross……you may lose your way."

"Okay…. that is so kind of him," said Mrs Housy.

Within ten minutes they reached the Dolphin beach.

The sight was arresting as hundreds of Dolphins were dancing to the music being played at the beach.

"Wow…. lovely," screamed the children.

The teachers too gave a surprised look.

Mr Single's words almost got stuck, "I have never seen so many Dolphins together."

The waves came splashing on them and they ran back and forth. The teachers indicated to them to stay away from water.

The girls sat on the rocks, and it was a feast for their eyes. Suddenly, a small boy in rags came running towards them and handed Roop a small piece of paper.

"What is this?" she inquired.

He pointed his hand in the direction of the lane from which they had come.

The girls shrieked as the same old lady whom they saw at Mr Pompey's house was standing and giving strange expressions to them.

Roop quickly opened the piece of paper. A small note was written in red.

She read it aloud, "Today midnight all the children will disappear…. WAIT AND WATCH."

CHAPTER FIVE

When the children looked back, she disappeared. The colour of their faces turned white as if the blood had been drained out. Roop and Vanya had seen her closely and they were sure that she was the same ghost.

The girls decided to discuss this matter further with their teachers. Roop simply nodded her head.

She said, "We will talk to our teachers tomorrow."

Mrs Housy called out, "Children let us go back. It's getting dark."

Meter was the one who lead the group. The girls were uncomfortable and they kept on looking hither and thither. They were afraid that the ghost may appear suddenly from any of the houses.

Mr Single asked the children, "I hope everything is fine. Something is bothering the girls."

Vanya replied in her shaky voice, "No Sir….no…no."

He halted and looked at their faces, "Okay…do share….if you feel like it. This place is new for all of us."

They walked back through the dark lanes and reached Pompey's house.

On the way, Meter declared, "The dinner will be laid in an hour or so. All of you be in the dining room by 8 o'clock."

The house was dimly lit and the dark clouds gathered. The weather was turning rough and suddenly it started raining heavily. All of them ran to find shelter but Roop thought this was the time when she could sneak into the house in the backyard.

She had to find an answer to the note which they got. Several questions arose in her mind.

"Why was she after the children? How was she related to Pompey? How did she resemble the lady in the portrait?"

She had to find an answer to these queries without troubling her teachers.

Roop saw that all of them were busy enjoying the rain. She quietly slipped out and hid behind a tree. It was pitch dark and the ground was wet. She pressed her shoes firmly to the muddy grass and moved towards the house.

Suddenly her right shoe got stuck in the mud, she tried to pull it out but failed. A hand came out from the darkness and pulled her out.

She almost screamed, "Who is it? Come and show your face."

Nobody turned up and the clouds thundered. She looked around but not a single soul was there. She could hear the faint voices of her friends.

She moved further and reached near the window. She tried to open it but it was tightly bolted. There was no light in that room. She reached near the door and tried to push it open.

Roop had heard stories of ghosts from her grandmother but her mother had explained that it was just a part of imagination.

The door was heavy and old fashioned. She knocked but there was a grave silence.

She heard the creaking of the door that opened on its own, and someone pulled her from inside. She fell

with a thud and badly hit her head. The door closed on
its own.

CHAPTER SIX

The rain stopped and all of them gathered in the corridor to go inside for dinner. The teachers started calling out their names. All the students were present but there was complete silence when Roop's name was called out.

Mrs Housy called again in a bit loud tone, "Roop…. Roop. Come back don't play games. Don't hide."

There was no response. There was a dead silence.

Mr Single said in a worried manner, "All of you go and check where is she hiding. We told her not to go far."

The boys and girls went in different directions. The girls gathered near the fountain.

Ruhi started sweating and said, "I think she must have fallen into some trap. We need to tell our teachers about the note we got on the beach. There is a ghost in this house.”

Vanya said pointing towards the house in the backyard, “She was the one who sent that note. I’m sure. There is a female ghost in this house.”

Ruhi enquired, “Are ghosts male or female?”

“She recognises us.She wants to kill the children. Oh!” said Juhi rubbing her cold hands.

Meter came out holding a few chappatis in his hand.

“Who will eat this?” inquired Mr Single.

“It is for the stray dogs,” he said moving towards the backyard.

“Do stray dogs enter your house at night?”

“No Sir,” said Meter and he was about to leave when Mrs Housy came and stood next to him.

She said, “One of our students Roop has still not come…..we know nothing about your house….. it’s so complicated……mathematical figures everywhere…..I think Roop must have got stuck in some cube or square.”

Meter stood dumbstruck and kept the chappatis in one corner. He started pulling his hair as if giving serious thought to the matter.

"Wait…Wait I will search for her…..come with me boys."

He started running all around calling out her name but the name simply echoed in the deep silence.

The girls came up to Mrs Housy and told the entire happenings of two days.

She asked the girls with her eyes bulging out, "Who is she? Where is that note?"

Vanya started trembling with fear, "Ma'am I saw her that night. She knocked on our window. She has long nails and hair. That note is with Roop."

Mrs Housy started sobbing, "Strange happenings are going on in this house. I don't believe in ghosts. Roop hardly listens to us. I didn't want to bring her. She is brave as well as arrogant. Oh! God let my child be safe."

The boys gave a faint smile on seeing Meter behaving awkwardly but were more worried about Roop.

"Where is she Meter? You stay in this house. What is all this? I think we should call Mr Pompey. Call your guards," shouted Mr Single.

Every nook and corner was searched but Roop was nowhere to be seen. Mrs Housy sat on the chair with a heavy heart and told Meter to call Mr Pompey

Roop could sense someone standing near her legs. The room was dark with an old-fashioned lamp flickering in one corner. Roop opened her right eye and saw the same ghost standing with a silver sword.

The ghost said with tears falling on Roop's legs, "Ha Ha Ha, that Pompey…. that silly mathematician is befooling me. I will put an end to his dirty business."

Roop closed her right eye tightly and thought, "Do ghosts cry? From her voice, she could make out that it was a female. She knew Pompey Plus quite well."

The ghost placed the sword on Roop's stomach and started rotating it. Her stomach started hurting but she pressed her teeth and lips tightly.

"Ha Ha Ha, thief……cheater….and you girl…. students….I hate students. You are in my custody finally. One by one all of you will come to me."

Roop had to think of a quick idea. She thought that the ghost is well known to Pompey and some deeper meaning lies behind it.

She caught hold of the sword and tried to move out. The ghost jumped on her and caught her by her hair.

Roop shouted, "Who are you? You are not a ghost. Leave me….please…..I'm innocent."

"No one of you will go back….I will drink your blood."

"No…..Please…..no…We were invited by Pompey Sir. My friends are waiting for me."

"I am a ghost. I will kill all of you. Don't call him sir. He doesn't deserve respect. Dirty old man"

Roop noticed her closely. She understood that she was a sufferer. She could hear her breathing heavily.

She was a living woman and not a ghost.

Roop gathered courage while trying to free her hair and in a thin voice cried, "Okay you are a ghost. Leave, my hair…. it's hurting….Do what you like….but listen to me first…..I will obey your orders."

"It's twenty years story and every day I wait for new children….I have caught many but somehow they escape."

Roop tried to please her now, "You can share your problem with me. Maybe, I can be of some help."

The ghost left her hair and walked away with large steps. She opened the glass window and looked out.

She placed her two hands with big nails behind her ears and said, "You can hear your name…. What is it? Roop…. Roop. They are searching for you but they can never find you."

Roop knew that all her teachers and friends must be worried but she had to find an answer to certain questions.

"Who was she? Why was she trying to kill children?"

She turned back to sit on her rocking chair. Roop noticed several mathematical exercises solved on the four walls of the room in the dim light. There were pens, pencils, coal and chalk lying everywhere.

Roop kept sitting on the floor and asked, "Can I call you aunty or mother? Can you switch on the light?"

The ghost started howling, "No let there be darkness…Oh, how I wish someone call me aunty…. but no….come to me, let me sharpen my sword…then chop off your head."

Roop came closer and held her harsh hand with big nails.

She asked gently, "Who are you?"

"My name….name….do I remember….yes…yes…I am a ghost about to kill you," she answered.

CHAPTER EIGHT

Mr Pompey Plus along with Meter rushed from inside in his oversized night suit. He walked with large steps and came to the end of the corridor. He went and stood near the two teachers then adjusted his thick spectacles and asked,

"What happened? Who has gone missing?"

Mr Single turned towards him with his nose swollen with anger and said in an obnoxious tone, "One of our students Roop has gone missing in your mathematical house. If we are unable to find her, we are going to file a complaint with the local police."

"Don't worry….see the walls of my house…guards," said he pointing towards the sky-touching walls ." "No one can enter or go out…Just wait…. Meter go and call centimetre……we need his help."

Meter obediently said, "Okay Sir," and ran inside. Within three minutes he returned holding the arms of a very old man with a black stick. His hands were shaking and he couldn't even raise his head properly.

Mrs Housy asked, "Who is he?"

Meter gave a quick answer, "My father Centimeter."

Mr Pompey went up to him and bent down up to his ear, "Well, Centimeter we need your help."

Centimeter held his right ear and tried to listen, "Yes…my lord……yes…. y…. e…s. What…… happened?"

Pompey explained, "One of the girls has gone missing…. Roop. She was standing in the garden when suddenly she vanished."

"What? Who? How? When?" said he shaking his head.

"Only you can help us we know."

All the students stood astonished when Mr Pompey said these words. How could an old man search for Roop?

Centimetre started nodding his head and looked at all the people standing there.

He said in a low voice, "Okay….again…. ….all of

you go inside…..I will try to bring her. I have told her so many times…spare the children."

Mr Pompey caught hold of his arm tightly as if trying to hurt him, "Don't utter a single word."

Mr Single said in a surprised manner, "What is he trying to tell?"

"Nothing…nothing…just speaking rubbish as he is old," said Mr Pompey, wiping his forehead's sweat.

Mrs Housy held his hand and begged, "We would be very grateful to you old man…..Mr Centimeter. Bring my child back…..she is not responding to any of us."

Mr Pompey took all of them inside. The girls started crying.

Centimeter moved forward with his stick towards the backyard. Meter accompanied him.

It had started drizzling again when they crossed the garden area.

They reached the small cottage in the backyard and knocked on the door.

CHAPTER NINE

"Open the door, Sylvia," said Centimetre in a loving shaky voice. "We love you……you will always be in the topmost position…..no one can beat you."

Meter too tried to push the door but it was bolted from inside. He requested, "Please open…please…I know she is with you…. leave the girl…don't be so stubborn and revengeful."

Roop could hear them, but she could not move from her position as the ghost made her sit on the floor in one corner of the room. The name Sylvia drew her attention as she quickly recalled the memories of the portrait in the classroom.

"Who was she? She resembled the lady in the picture" thought Roop. She tried to get up, but the ghost continuously gave her a wicked smile.

She gained courage and asked, "Are you, Sylvia? See somebody is calling your name. They want you to open the door."

The ghost pierced her nails into her cheeks and shrieked with tears in her eyes, "Who is Sylvia? Who are you to ask my name? I don't remember my name."

Roop saw Meter from the glass window but she could not recognize the old man. She shouted, "Help! Help! Meter I am here…..Save me from the ghost….. she is trying to kill me."

Meter could not hear as the windows were closed. They had started banging on the door. The ghost tried to tie a cloth on her mouth and eyes. Roop struggled hard but could not escape.

The door flung open in the meantime and the ghost turned towards it to have a look at Meter.

Meter quickly entered and opened the cloth tied to Roop's eyes and mouth. Roop noticed that the ghost remained quite normal and it seemed she was well known to these people.

They screamed, "Stop….stop….don't harm this blameless girl."

She threw her hands from Roop and said in a hoarse voice, "Why? It's been twenty years now…..I have lost my youth, and my children…. my mind has become dumped. Why do you come again and again? Don't disturb me. This fat, old ugly Pompey deserves punishment."

Centimetre walked slowly in the dim light and freed Roop from her clutches. She rushed towards meter.

Centimetre gently caught her arm and tried to convince her, "Sylvia…..Sylvia Matrix….we are helpless. Look at my condition…I have grown weak and sick but I could not help you, my love. I am a sinner. Punish me but not innocent children."

The ghost gave a venomous sneer, "I am not listening to you now…stop."

Roop was shocked to hear such conversations between a ghost and the two.

He gently pushed her with his stick. Meter switched on the lights and Roop saw that the room was small and dirty. Mugs, plates and food too were scattered on the floor.

She saw scenes which were difficult to digest. She thought, "There was some connection among the three."

Meter was holding Sylvia's hands and calling her, "Mother…. mother…. please….stop….for my sake. Something will be done …don't worry. I am always there when you call me. I obey your orders.I even wear your clothes and act as a ghost…..remember on the beach Roop.”

He hugged her tightly and Sylvia started howling. Roop was silently watching all this. She came forward with a bold step and asked, “Okay….I thought how could she reach on the beach…If I am not mistaken you are Sylvia Matrix……the great mathematician…. Ghost Sylvia Matrix…..I saw your portrait in the classroom.”

Meter caught hold of Centimeter and made him sit on the chair. Sylvia went up to him and kept her head in his lap.

“When will we start living like a happy family again? I love you both.”

“If you don’t mind, can I help you……I have a great plan.”

Meter and Centimeter entered the living room with Roop hale and hearty in half an hour. The teachers and students stood up and gathered around her.

Mr Pompey Plus gave a wicked smile on seeing them. He patted her cheeks with his heavy hands and said, "See she is back…..safe and sound….all of you created so much confusion…my house looked like hell for a few moments."

Ruhi and Vanya hugged her tightly and asked, "Did the ghost try to kill you?"

"No there is no ghost…..I got stuck in the thorny bushes and it was so kind of them to help me," she said pointing towards Meter and Centimeter.

Mrs Housy handed her a glass of water and said, "We knew you would be back. All of you see she is such a brave girl. Meter ordered, "Come on wash your hands' children. It's dinner time."

After dinner, Roop requested all her friends and teachers to come to her room as she wanted to narrate the entire incident.

Mr Pompey Plus grew suspicious then with both, hands on his waist asked, "Can I join you?"

Roop gave a sly look and said, "No Sir, there is nothing special to tell."

He simply rubbed his hands and went away. All of them had a great time when Roop told them the real story of the ghost of Aunt Sylvia Matrix. In the end, she pleaded, "Please let it be a secret for two more days."

On the sixth day, the bus was ready in the morning at eight. Smarty dragged all the suitcases and kept them in the compartment while the children carried their handbags. They were overjoyed as they had learnt a few secret formulas in mathematics.

The children had breakfast with Mr Pompey although he took leave as he had some urgent appointment.

Mr Single called out their names and one by one the students entered the bus. They settled themselves well as they had to cover a distance of three hundred kilometres. The guards entered the bus and checked it thoroughly.

The gates of the mathematical house were opened and they all sighed in relief.

After half an hour the bus halted on the roadside as soon as they reached the highway. All of them got down and Smarty climbed to the top of the bus.

The students started clapping as Centimeter, Meter, and Sylvia Matrix got down with Smarty's help. They took them onto the bus and gave them water. They looked tired and worn out but smiled at being free after twenty long years.

They stepped into the bus and relaxed in the front seats. Smarty served them wafers and biscuits.

Mrs Sylvia Matrix stood up and turned towards the students as well as teachers. She looked so dissimilar and there was no fear.

She folded her hands and said with tears flowing down her eyes, "I am left with no words…. I am thankful…. grateful….to all but especially to Roop without whose help my family wouldn't have been here today."

She signalled Roop to come forward as she was seated in the back seat. Roop came up to her and Sylvia hugged her tightly.

She wiped her tears then smiled and said, "If all of you hadn't rescued me and hidden me on the bus last night, I would have died of loneliness and failure in life. Twenty years back we were invited by Mr Pompey for a two-day stay. He wanted to congratulate me personally as I had won a National Award for mathematics but we were unaware of all this. He kept threatening us that if we try to escape he would put an end to our life."

The teachers stood aghast, "What? For twenty years you had been kidnapped."

"Things and situations have changed….I am no more afraid. He was jealous of me….my husband Centimeter and son Meter accompanied me and they too have suffered as they had to work like servants…. my passion for my subject was lost…. I was left like a zombie….I developed a hatred for children who study this subject. Roop is a brave girl. She was not afraid of me from the first day. I am finally going home now."

Mr Single said, "You told us your home was on the way and we will safely drop you there."

"Today because of your efforts I will reach home. My people have thought that I am dead. Thank you to all."

The bus slowly moved forward.